Prime Time Adventures

CAVE-IN!

By Lael Littke

Illustrated by Tom Dunnington

 CHILDRENS PRESS, CHICAGO

Library of Congress Cataloging in Publication Data

Littke, Lael.
  Cave-in!

  (Prime time adventures)
  SUMMARY: When her brother gets lost in a cave and two
friends disappear trying to find him, Janet desperately
searches for a way out of their predicament.
  [[1. Rescue work—Fiction. 2. Caves—Fiction]
I. Dunnington, Tom. II. Title.
PZ7.L719Cav   [Fic]   80-28189
ISBN 0-516-02102-8

CONTENTS

1   TROUBLE AT FIREHOLE CREEK   1

2   WATER IN THE CAVE   7

3   ALONE!   15

4   HELP!   19

5   THE END OF THE ROPE   25

6   HIGH WATER   33

7   A CLOUD OF BATS   39

8   DOWN THE ICY WATERFALL   47

9   IN DARKNESS AGAIN   55

CHAPTER 1

TROUBLE AT FIREHOLE CREEK

Janet looked out of the car. She saw dark clouds in the sky.

"I hope it doesn't rain," she said. "That would spoil our picnic."

Rick steered the car carefully. The mountain road was narrow. "We won't have a picnic if it rains. We'll just pick up Steve and Charlie. Then we'll go back home."

"Couldn't we sit under a tree?" Janet asked. "I brought a lot of food. I'm hungry."

Rick smiled at her. "I am, too," he said. "But storms can be dangerous in these mountains. You haven't lived around here very long. You don't know how bad they can be."

"Well, then can't we just stay in the car and eat?" Janet said. "That should be safe enough."

"No," Rick said. "A lot of rain might wash out this road. We wouldn't be able to get out of here." He looked worried. Big raindrops began to hit the car. "I hope Steve and Charlie are waiting for us. I don't want to stay any longer than we have to."

"They said they would be there at noon," Janet told him.

Steve was her brother. Charlie was Steve's friend. They had been on a backpack trip. Three days ago Janet and Rick had taken them to their starting place. Today they were supposed to pick them up at Firehole Creek. It was almost fifty miles back in the mountains. Janet wanted to have a picnic before they started back. But now Rick said no.

Janet liked Rick a lot. She hoped he liked her. That's why she didn't say she thought he worried too much. The rain didn't look too bad.

"Maybe it will stop soon," she said.

"I don't think so." Rick turned the car down a bumpy road that led to Firehole Creek. "Do you see Steve and Charlie?"

"No," Janet said. "But I see their tents. They must have camped here last night. Maybe they're still asleep."

Rick pulled into a clearing. He stopped next to two small tents. He and Janet got out of the car. They went to look inside the tents. The backpacks were there. But Steve and Charlie were not.

"I wonder where they are," Rick said.

Suddenly they heard running footsteps. Charlie ran into the clearing.

"I'm glad you're here," he said. He stopped to catch his breath.

He looked scared. That frightened Janet. "Where is my brother?" she asked.

"Now take it easy," Charlie said. "I think he's all right. But I can't find him."

"Can't find him!" Rick said. "What happened to him?"

"I think he's in a cave." Charlie pointed back up the mountain behind him. "We decided to walk up there this morning. There are a lot of caves. We went inside one. Steve didn't come out."

"Those caves are not safe to go into," Rick said. "There are signs all over saying you should stay out. Didn't you see them?"

Charlie hung his head. "Don't get mad, Rick. We thought we would go in just a little way. But it was interesting. We kept on going.

Then Steve went down one tunnel and I went down another.''

"For crying out loud, how dumb can you get?'' Rick said. "You should never be alone in a cave. You must have someone with you. Did you call Steve's name? Did you look for him?''

"Sure, I did,'' Charlie said. "But he didn't answer. I think he's all right. He had a good flashlight. The batteries in mine are almost worn out. That's why I came out to look for you. I couldn't stay in there without a good light.''

"You should have thought of that before you went in,'' Rick said. "Well, we'll have to go back to a town. We need more help.'' He started toward the car.

Janet didn't want to leave. She wasn't too worried about Steve. He was probably just walking around in the cave looking at things. But Rick had said a storm in the mountains was dangerous. They should find Steve as soon as possible.

"Wouldn't it take a lot of time to go after more help?'' she asked. "Can't we go look for Steve now?''

Rick stopped. "We don't have the things we

need to go into a cave. We need ropes. We need strong lights. We need warm clothes. We should have hard hats and good boots.''

''I have a long rope in my pack,'' Charlie said. ''Steve and I thought we might need it for mountain climbing.''

''We have our jackets,'' Janet said. ''And you always carry a good flashlight in your car, Rick. Couldn't we use that? It's raining really hard now. You said the road might wash out. Don't you think we should find Steve before that happens?''

Rick looked up at the dark sky. ''I guess you're right.'' He turned to Charlie. ''Bring your rope. I'll get my flashlight from the car.''

Soon they were ready to go. Rick led the way into the trees.

''I'm not sure I can find the right cave again,'' Charlie said. ''It had a big opening. And there was a little tree right by it.''

''I'll find it,'' Rick said. ''I've been here with my father. He and some other men were checking the caves. They wanted to see if they are safe for people to go in. They decided they are not. So they put up the signs.''

It made Janet feel better to know that Rick had been in the caves. They might find Steve fast. She looked around as they climbed the mountain. There didn't seem to be any trail.

"How do you know which way to go?" she asked.

"You look for landmarks," Rick said. "See that big rock over there? You know you are halfway when you pass it. Then you head for that tall tree up there."

No one said much more as they climbed. The rain was getting worse. It was hard going.

Then suddenly they were there. The opening to the cave was very large. It looked as if it were ready to swallow them. Janet was afraid. Her brother was in there. Somewhere in that dark cave.

Rick stood looking at the cave. He didn't seem to want to go in. "Maybe he has already come out," he said. "Maybe he has already started down the mountain."

"I don't think so," Charlie said. He walked over to something red just inside the cave. He picked it up. "This is his jacket," he said. "He would have taken it if he had come out. He's still in there."

CHAPTER **2**

WATER IN THE CAVE

They all stood there in the rain. They looked at the jacket.

"Why didn't Steve take his jacket with him?" Rick asked. "It's cold in the cave."

"Yes," Charlie said. "We found that out. But we got hot climbing the mountain. We dropped our jackets here before we went in."

"Rick," Janet said, "we had better find Steve fast. I heard somewhere that it's dangerous to get too cold."

"It is." Rick shined his flashlight around the cave opening. "If a person loses too much body heat, he doesn't think clearly."

"Then what happens?" Janet could feel her heart beating fast.

Rick shook his head. "I don't know. Almost anything. Let's just get in there and start looking."

He took the rope Charlie had carried. He tied one end of it to the little tree by the cave opening. He put the rest of it over his shoulder. "There are a lot of tunnels in there," he said. "I'll let the rope out as we go along. Then we can always find our way out. Now, Charlie, show us where you last saw Steve."

He shined his light inside the cave. Charlie led the way. They all went in. The floor of the cave slanted down. Rain was running in. Janet slipped. She almost fell. Rick grabbed her arm and held her up.

Janet didn't like the cave. It wasn't high enough for them to stand up. They had to bend over a little. It was dark and wet and cold.

Charlie stopped when they came to a small tunnel. It branched off to the left. "We stopped here," he said. "Stick your head in. You will hear water splashing. We wondered if there might be a waterfall. We talked about going in there. But we decided to wait until we came back."

"It's a good thing you changed your minds," Rick said. "You have to go into that one on your hands and knees. It's called a crawl." He bent down. He shined his light inside. "Look. There is a big rock hanging down from the roof. You would have a hard time getting past it."

Janet got down so she could see. She could hear water falling somewhere. Steve liked waterfalls.

Then she saw the marks in the dirt. The floor of the crawl was not as low as the tunnel they were in. The rain didn't run in there, so the marks were plain.

"Rick," she said. "It looks as if someone has been in here."

Rick pointed his light at the marks. "Did you two go in there at all, Charlie?"

Charlie looked in, too. "No. But maybe Steve went in after I left."

"I've never been in that crawl," Rick said. "I don't know what is in there. I wouldn't want to go in without better lights."

That worried Janet. "Rick, Steve may be in trouble in there. We can't go back after better lights now."

Rick looked around the crawl again. "Steve might have gone in there. But he probably got only as far as the rock. Let's go look around in other parts of the cave. If we don't find him, then I'll look in the crawl."

Janet could see that Rick didn't want to go into the crawl. "Couldn't we just call to him in there right now?" she asked.

"It's worth a try," Rick said.

He pulled Janet and Charlie close to the crawl. They all screamed, "Steve! Steve!"

Their voices echoed in the cave.

No one answered.

"OK, Charlie," Rick said. "Take us to where you and Steve went down different tunnels."

Charlie started to go down into the cave. Rick followed. There was nothing for Janet to do but go with them. But she kept thinking about the crawl.

They slipped along until they came to another tunnel. Charlie pointed to the right.

"That's where Steve went. I stayed in this one we are in," he said. "Then my light got dim and I left."

The tunnel Steve had taken was very narrow. They started down it. But Rick's light wasn't strong enough. They had a hard time seeing. They stumbled along for a while. Then Rick said, "This isn't going to work. One light isn't enough for three people. Let's go back to the crawl. Then I'll tell you what we'll do."

They made their way back to the crawl. Janet hoped they were going to go into it. But when they got there, Rick said, "You two wait here. It will be dark. But it's out of the rain. I'll take the light. I'll go as far as my rope will reach."

He turned and went back down the tunnel. Janet and Charlie watched him go.

"I think we should have gone into the crawl," Charlie said. "Do you think Rick is chicken?"

"I don't know," Janet said. "He worries about a lot of things. But I don't see why we can't go a little way into the crawl."

Charlie took his flashlight out of his pocket. He turned it on. "My light is dim. But I'll go in there. Then I can see what is on the other side of the rock."

"I'll go, too," Janet said. "You go first. Then shine the light back for me."

Charlie got down on his hands and knees. He went into the crawl. Janet could hear him moving along. The only other sound was the loud waterfall somewhere deep inside.

"Wait out there," Charlie called back. "I don't know if I can get past this rock. It hangs down almost to the floor."

Janet heard some noises. Then Charlie called, "I made it." He was on the other side of the rock. Janet was in the dark by herself.

"I'm coming now," she called.

Charlie didn't answer for a minute. Janet could hear her heart beating. "Charlie," she called. "Are you there?"

Then she heard him. "Janet," he said, "I'm sure Steve has been here. I just found a gum wrapper. Steve chews gum all the time. I think he must have dropped it here."

"That's great, Charlie," Janet said. "I'm coming in, too."

She started crawling on her hands and knees. She heard Charlie coming back to the big rock. She saw the flash of his light.

"I'll stay on this side," he said. "Then I can shine my light so you can see how to get around the rock."

Janet crawled as far as the rock. It was a strange, small, dark place. It was like being buried in a small space.

"I can't get past the rock," Janet said. "I'm afraid."

"Try to get under it," Charlie told her. "After you pass the rock, the tunnel is a lot bigger. You won't be afraid in here."

Janet tried to push herself under the rock. It
moved a little.

"The rock moved," she said. "Do you think
we could pull it out of the roof? It would be a
lot easier to move if it was gone."

She saw Charlie shine his weak light on the
rock. "Yes. Maybe I could get it out. I could
pull it in here where I am."

He began pulling on it with his free hand. Janet pushed on it from her side.

"It would work better if you held the light," Charlie said. "Then I could see what I'm doing."

He passed the light around the rock to her. She pointed it where it would help him. She heard him pulling at the big rock.

"It's coming," he said.

The rock came out suddenly. A lot of dirt fell on Janet's head. She backed up.

Suddenly the whole roof where the rock had been caved in. All Janet could see in the dim light was a wall of dirt.

Charlie was on the other side of it.

Or maybe he was under it.

"Charlie!" Janet screamed. "Are you all right?"

She listened. She couldn't hear him answer. She couldn't even hear the waterfall any more.

The crawl was as silent as a grave.

CHAPTER 3
ALONE !

"Charlie!" Janet screamed again.

She put the flashlight down. She began to dig at the wall of dirt with her fingers. But there was too much of it.

She had to get to Charlie. He might be hurt.

But how was she going to do that? She didn't have anything to dig with.

She thought of Rick. He would be angry because she and Charlie hadn't listened to him. They should never have gone into the crawl. But that didn't matter now. Janet had to find Rick. He would know what to do.

Janet picked up the flashlight. She tried to turn around. There wasn't enough room. She would have to back out.

Slowly she crawled back. She couldn't see where she was going. The rocks on the cave floor hurt her hands and knees.

15

Soon she was back in the bigger tunnel. She shined the weak flashlight around. She saw Rick's rope. All she had to do was follow the rope and she would find Rick.

The light was so dim now that she could hardly see. The batteries would soon be dead. She took hold of the rope.

The rope led Janet down, down, down. She went deeper and deeper into the earth. She came to where other tunnels turned off. They led to the left and right. But the rope led her the right way. The tunnel was bigger now. She could stand up.

Water was coming in from the sides of the cave. Janet thought it must be raining harder outside. She wondered what would happen if it flooded the cave.

"Rick!" she called.

Her voice echoed around the cave. It sounded as if she were in a bigger place now.

Suddenly she heard a strange sound. Something hit her face. She turned the flashlight up. She saw something that looked like a bird. Then another, and another. But what would birds be doing deep in a cave?

Then she knew what they were. Bats! She was in a cave of bats!

Janet turned to run out of the cave. But then she stopped. She couldn't go out before she found Rick. She had to go on.

Bats flew all around her. It was like a nightmare.

She stood still for a few minutes. She watched the bats. They went on down the tunnel where she was heading. She wondered why they went that way. Perhaps there was another way out down there.

Janet took a deep breath. She started following the rope again. She was quiet this time. It must have been her shouting that woke the bats. She wouldn't do that again.

The rope took her into a large tunnel. But the water in there was about six inches deep. It was very cold. It splashed as she walked. She had to move fast before it got any higher.

Then she thought of something. Rick was carrying the rope. If she pulled on it, he would feel it. He would know something was wrong. Then he would start back toward her. That would save time.

Janet put the flashlight under her arm. That way she could use both hands to pull on the rope. A good hard yank or two would tell Rick to come fast.

She pulled hard. But she couldn't feel anything on the end of the rope.

What had happened to Rick?

She held the flashlight in one hand. She held the rope in the other. She didn't pull again. She had to find out where the end was.

It didn't take long. The tunnel went to the left. The end of the rope was just around the corner.

But Rick was not there. The rope floated on top of the water.

"Rick!" she called. She didn't care now if she scared up any bats.

She stood still to listen. Far off she heard something like a waterfall. But that was all.

She wondered if the waterfall was the same one they had heard from the crawl. Rick must have come to the end of the rope. Then he must have gone on to find the waterfall.

Janet could hardly see any more. The light was getting weaker. She had to get out of the cave. She didn't have enough light. She couldn't look any farther for Rick.

She started back along the rope. It was like a lifeline leading her back to the world.

She had just reached the bat cave when the flashlight went out completely.

CHAPTER **4**

HELP !

Janet screamed. She couldn't hold it back.
She was alone in a cave full of water. And she
had no light! She didn't know the way out.
Only the rope in her hand could lead her back.

Her screams scared the bats. They flew
about her head. They were making strange,
high noises. One of them got caught in her
hair. She put up both hands to get it away.
That made her drop the rope. She felt around
in the icy water for it. If she lost the rope, she
would never get out.

When she found it, she held it with both
hands. She didn't care if bats got in her hair.
That was better than being lost.

She hung onto the rope. She began to move
forward. She slipped and stumbled through
the bat cave. Finally she was back in the
narrow tunnel. She could hear water coming

19

through the cracks in the cave walls. It was cold. Her feet were numb.

She didn't know when she passed the crawl where Charlie was trapped. She couldn't see anything in the dark. She began to talk to herself. "It will be all right," she told herself. "I'll soon be out."

It seemed like hours before she saw daylight. Then she was outside. She was standing in the rain. She stood there for a moment, letting it fall on her face. It was warmer than the water inside the cave.

She wanted to fall to the ground and rest. But she couldn't. She had to get to the car. She had to find help.

She looked around through the rain. She didn't even know which way to go. Then she remembered that Rick had pointed out some landmarks. "The tall tree," he had said.

Janet looked until she saw the tall tree. She ran down the mountain toward it. Then she saw the big rock Rick had showed her. She went to it. From there it wasn't hard to find her way back to Firehole Creek. The car was there. Nothing had ever looked so good to her. She would get in it and drive to the next town. She would find someone there who would help.

She ran to the car. She pulled on the door. It was locked. Rick had the keys.

"Oh, no," Janet said out loud. She felt like crying. She stood there wondering what she was going to do.

She had to do something. But there wasn't much she could do. She started walking along the narrow road. Maybe she would find someone.

But who would be out in all this rain? Streams of water were running across the road now. No one would want to drive on roads like this. She wondered if she could walk to the nearest town. It had to be at least ten miles away.

Then she saw the green truck. She thought she must be dreaming. But she heard the sound of its motor. That couldn't be a dream!

Janet ran toward the truck. There were some words on its side. They said "United States Forest Service."

"Stop!" she screamed.

The driver saw her. He stopped. He got out of the truck.

"What's the matter, Sis?" he asked.

"The cave," Janet cried. "My brother and my friends are lost in a cave."

The man didn't ask questions. He just said, "Get in my truck. I'll drive as close as I can to the cave. We'll find your brother and your friends, Sis."

He was a big man. He looked a little like Janet's father. She would let him take over the search. He could probably find the boys fast.

"I'm so glad you came," she said. "I was afraid I wouldn't find anyone to help."

"We always check these back roads when it storms," the man said. He started the truck. He drove carefully through the rain. "Sometimes the rain washes out the road. Then people get into trouble."

Janet looked out at the rain. She was shaking. She realized her clothes were cold and wet. "That's what Rick said," she told the man. "He said we should get out of here fast."

"He's a smart boy," the man said. "By the way, my name is Al Brady. I'm with the Forest Service. Now, why don't you tell me which cave the boys are in. And how they got lost in there. You should not have gone in there at all, you know."

"I know," Janet said. Then she told him how Steve and Charlie had gone in. She told him the whole story about the cave-in. And she told him about how she couldn't find Rick. "Charlie said it was the biggest cave here," she finished. "There is a small tree by the opening."

"I think I know which one it is," Mr. Brady said. "But I haven't been in those caves much. I'll see if I can radio for more help as soon as we stop."

It was hard for him to keep the truck on the road. It slipped around in the mud. In some places the rain had filled deep holes. Mr. Brady tried to drive around them. But sometimes the wheels went right into them. Then the truck almost stopped.

"If we can keep going, we'll get close to the cave," Mr. Brady said. "We are on a Forest Service road. It goes almost all the way there."

Janet was glad she didn't have to climb the hill again. She was tired. But there was no time to rest.

"Do you have some lights?" she asked. "We'll need a shovel to dig away the dirt that caved in on Charlie."

"I have two good lights," Mr. Brady said. "And we'll take a short-handled backpack shovel. I also have a lot of rope. We'll need that in the cave.''

That made Janet think of Rick and his rope. She wondered why he had gone farther than the end of it. She was thinking of that when Mr. Brady stopped the truck.

''This is as far as we can go,'' he said. He pointed outside. ''The road is washed out up ahead.''

''Let's start walking then,'' Janet said. ''I just want to get back to the cave. We have to find the boys fast.''

Mr. Brady nodded. ''First let me call for more help, Sis.''

He pushed some buttons on his radio. ''Ranger Two, Ranger Two,'' he said. ''Come in.''

There was a lot of static. But that was all.

He pushed some more buttons. ''Come in,'' he said. ''Come in anyone.''

There was more static and crackling.

Mr. Brady turned to Janet. ''Sometimes the radio doesn't work too well in these mountains. Especially when it rains like this.''

He put his hand on the door handle. ''Let's go, Sis,'' he said. ''I guess it's up to you and me.''

CHAPTER **5**

THE END OF THE ROPE

Janet got out of the truck. She looked at the wet trees. "I don't know which way to go," she said.

"Don't worry, Sis," Mr. Brady said. "I'll find it. But first I want you to put on a dry shirt. I always keep some clean shirts in the truck."

"That will take too much time," Janet said.

But Mr. Brady was already at the back of the truck. He was opening up a chest. "No way, Sis. You're already wet from the rain. The cave is cold. You can't take a chance on getting too cold in there." He pulled out a dark green Forest Service shirt. He also took out two raincoats. Then he locked the chest again.

"Get into the truck and put these on," he said. He handed her the shirt and a raincoat. "They will help a lot."

Janet did as he said. Rick had told her how dangerous it was to get cold. She had to be able to think clearly.

The shirt was much too big for her. But it felt good to be partly dry again. And it was nice to have a raincoat.

Janet got out of the truck. Mr. Brady was wearing the other raincoat. He was carrying a long rope. He also had a short-handled shovel and a package covered in plastic.

"What is that?" Janet asked. She pointed at the package.

"Blankets," Mr. Brady said. "Your brother and your friends will be cold. We have to have something to warm them."

That scared Janet again. Steve had been in the cave a long time. And he had left his jacket outside.

"Let's go," she said.

Mr. Brady gave her two big flashlights to carry. "Come this way," he said.

Janet followed him. They walked through the rain. It wasn't long until they came to the mouth of the cave.

"Show me which way each one went," Mr. Brady said. "Then we'll decide what to do first." He took one of the flashlights. He turned it on. Janet turned on the other one.

She didn't really want to go back into that wet, dark cave. But she had to. Mr. Brady wouldn't know where to look for the boys.

Janet bent over. She started into the cave. "This is the rope Rick used," she said, pointing to the rope.

"He has a lot of sense," Mr. Brady said. "He will probably be OK."

Janet wished she and Charlie had used

some sense. They should not have gone into the crawl. But it was too late to think about that now.

She led the way to the crawl.

"That's where the cave-in is," she said. "Charlie is on the other side of all that dirt." She told Mr. Brady about the gum wrapper Charlie had found. "Steve chews gum all the time. He could have dropped that wrapper. So he might be in there, too."

Mr. Brady pointed his light into the crawl. He looked inside. He put down the blankets and the rope. He got down on his hands and knees.

"I don't think I can get in there," he said. "I'm too big. We'll have to get in there another way."

"Do you know another way in?" Janet asked hopefully.

"No, Sis," Mr. Brady said. "Like I told you, I haven't been in these caves much. But there must be another way to get to that crawl."

Janet's heart sank. It wasn't going to be easy to find the boys. Even with Mr. Brady's help.

"Maybe we should look for Rick first," she said. "Maybe he has found something."

"Is he the one who used the rope?" Mr. Brady asked.

"Yes," Janet said.

Mr. Brady said, "Let's follow the rope on down. Maybe Rick has come back to it by now."

He picked up the things he had brought. Then he started off. Janet moved along behind him. They went through the bat cave. Then they went into the bigger tunnel. The water was almost up to Janet's knees now. Rick's rope floated on top of the water. They could see the end of it. It was a little way down the tunnel.

"That isn't where I found the end of the rope before," Janet said. "It was around a bend."

Mr. Brady walked through the water. He reached the end of the rope. "It probably floated here," he said. "That means he may not be able to find his way back here. We'll have to go down each tunnel and call him."

Janet pointed ahead to where the tunnel turned. "We should start there. That's where the end of the rope was before."

They walked around the bend of the tunnel.

"Rick!" Mr. Brady called.

They listened for an answer. All they could hear was the waterfall. It seemed very far off.

"Maybe he went to look for the waterfall," Janet said. "His rope wouldn't reach that far. Maybe he thought he could find his way back to it."

"Why would he want to find the waterfall?" Mr. Brady asked.

"We could hear the waterfall in the crawl," Janet told him. "Charlie said Steve was interested in the waterfall. Maybe Rick thought Steve came this way looking for it."

"Or maybe he thought he could find another way to the crawl," Mr. Brady said. "You could hear the waterfall in both places. There might be a connection."

"That's true," Janet said. "Can we go look at where the waterfall is?"

"Yes." Mr. Brady picked up the end of Rick's rope. He tied one end of his own rope to it. "This way we won't get lost, too," he said.

They started toward the sound of the waterfall.

Before long they came to a small cave. A waterfall splashed down one side of it. Then it disappeared. It went into a hole that went down even deeper.

Janet shined her light around. Rick was not there.

"He isn't here," she said. "I hoped we would find him."

Mr. Brady shined his light up. He tried to see where the waterfall came from. "He probably decided he couldn't get anywhere from here. I would say he went back to look for his rope."

"Can you see anything up there?" Janet asked.

Mr. Brady shook his head. "No. But it sounds like the water falls a long way. Maybe there is an outside opening to it." He turned around. "We'll try some other tunnels. Rick must be in one of them."

They followed the rope back. They reached the place where it was tied to Rick's rope. They saw another tunnel on the right. They went into it. They called, "Rick! Rick!"

There was no answer. They tried another tunnel.

"Rick! Rick!" they shouted.

This time they heard something. It came from a long way off. It sounded like someone calling "Help! Help! Help!"

Janet strained her ears to hear. Was it one voice? Or was it three? It couldn't be three. She knew Charlie was in the crawl.

She listened again. It was just one voice. But whose voice was it? Steve's? Or Rick's?

CHAPTER 6

HIGH WATER

"Can you tell which one of the boys that is?" asked Mr. Brady.

"No," Janet said. "He's too far away."

Mr. Brady started walking through the water. "Whoever he is, we should go to him. He sounds as if he's in trouble."

Janet followed him. "I hoped Rick had found Steve. I thought they might be together."

"I don't think so, Sis," Mr. Brady said. "It sounds like just one voice."

"Maybe they are together," Janet said. "Maybe one of them is hurt." She was shaking. Partly from the icy cold water. Partly because she was afraid.

"Don't think about it, Sis," Mr. Brady said. "Don't think up bad things before they happen."

He put up a hand to tell her to stop.

"Let's listen again," he said. "I can't tell where the voice is coming from."

They stopped. All they could hear was running water. It was getting deeper.

"Rick!" Janet screamed. "Steve!"

Mr. Brady shouted, too.

"Help!" the voice called again.

"Keep calling!" Mr. Brady shouted. "We'll come to you."

Again the voice shouted "Help! Help!"

"I think he's down there." Janet pointed to a tunnel that slanted down. The water was running into it very fast.

Mr. Brady made sure that his rope was still tied to Rick's. Then he ran over to the tunnel. Janet went, too. They listened again.

"Help!" the voice called. "The tunnel is filling up with water."

"It's Rick," Janet said to Mr. Brady. "I can tell his voice now." She called into the tunnel. "Rick, is Steve with you?"

"No," Rick called back. Then he shouted, "I need help. I can't move or I'll be washed away."

"I'll have to go after him," Mr. Brady said. "I'll need to hang onto the rope. But that tree

Rick's rope is tied to is small. I don't know if it's strong enough to hold me. Maybe I should go back and test it."

"No," Janet said. "I have an idea. Why don't you just let the rope float on the water? The water might carry it to where Rick is. Then you could stay here and pull him out."

"You're pretty smart, Sis," Mr. Brady said. "We can try that."

Mr. Brady took the rope from his shoulder. He let the end of it float on the water. It floated as far as a bend in the tunnel. Then it got caught on a rock.

"It won't work," Janet said. "Maybe I'm not so smart."

"Sure you are, Sis." Mr. Brady pulled the rope back. "But we need to tie something onto it. Something that is a little heavier than the rope. Something that will float." He looked around at what they had.

"How about one of our plastic raincoats?" Janet asked. She started to take hers off.

"That will do it," Mr. Brady said. "I'll fold it. I'll try to trap some air inside. But we'll use mine, not yours."

He folded his raincoat. He made sure there was a pocket of air inside. He tied the end of the rope to it. Then he let it float into the tunnel.

He and Janet watched it float around the bend.

"Rick!" Mr. Brady shouted into the tunnel. "Watch for a green plastic raincoat. There is a rope tied around it. Grab the rope. Tie it around you. Then we'll pull you up."

"Right," Rick called back.

They were all quiet then. The only noise was the sound of the water.

"Maybe it's caught again," Janet said. "Maybe it won't get to him."

"Wait and see, Sis," Mr. Brady said. "Remember what I told you? Don't think up bad things before they happen."

It seemed they waited a long time. Finally, Rick shouted, "It's here!"

A few more minutes went by. Then the rope moved. "I'm ready," Rick called.

Mr. Brady started to pull. Janet got behind him. She pulled, too. Pretty soon they could see Rick. He came around the bend of the tunnel. He was wearing the raincoat. He was hanging onto the rope. He still had his light.

Mr. Brady and Janet kept pulling. Soon Rick was right beside them.

Rick reached out his hands to touch them. "I'm sure glad to see you," he said.

Janet took hold of his hand. "We are glad to see you, too, Rick. Did you find any clues? About Steve I mean?"

"No," Rick said. "Let's go look for him now. How did you and Charlie know you should come after me?" He shined his light at Mr. Brady. "Oh," he said. "I thought you were Charlie."

"My name is Al Brady. I'm with the Forest Service. The young lady here flagged me down."

"But where is Charlie then?" Rick asked.

Janet told him how the crawl roof had caved in. She told him how she had gone out and found Mr. Brady.

Rick didn't say she and Charlie had been dumb to go in that crawl. He just said, "Mr. Brady, I'm sure glad you're here. We can use all the help we can get. Now we should try to get to Charlie. Maybe he has found Steve."

He started to take off the raincoat. But Mr. Brady told him to keep it.

"We need to decide what we are going to do," Mr. Brady said. "But first let's go back to the bat cave. The water isn't as high there."

Mr. Brady untied his rope from Rick's. He put it over his shoulder. Then they all followed Rick's rope. It led them back to the bat cave.

When they were there, Janet said, "I followed your rope to the end. I was afraid when you were not there."

"I heard the waterfall in that tunnel," Rick said. "The rope wasn't long enough to take me there. I spotted some landmarks and left my rope. When I came back, the water had washed it away. That's when I got lost."

"That's what we thought," Mr. Brady said. "Sis here told me why you wanted to get to the waterfall. Did you find any tunnels that connect it to the crawl?"

"No," Rick said. "But there has to be a connection." He shined his light around the cave. There were hundreds of bats on the roof. "Some bats flew past me when I was at the waterfall," he said. "This must be where they sleep."

"Never mind that," Janet said. "Do you have any idea at all where we can look for Steve?"

"Let's hope he's in the crawl with Charlie," Rick said. "There are all kinds of tunnels here. It would take days to search them all."

CHAPTER **7**

A Cloud of Bats

Janet felt sick. "That could be too late, couldn't it?"

Rick didn't say anything.

"Well now," said Mr. Brady, "let's not give up hope yet. Let's see if we can get into that crawl. We'll find out if he's in there with the other boy."

"Yes," Rick said. "That's the first thing to do. Charlie must be pretty scared in there. He has no light. If he didn't find Steve, that is."

Janet didn't tell him the dirt might have fallen on Charlie. Instead she said, "Rick, Mr. Brady thinks there might be another way to get to the crawl."

"I don't think we can dig our way through from this end," Mr. Brady said.

"I think the crawl must connect with the waterfall," Rick said. "But we need to find an outside opening to the waterfall. Then we could get there. Again it might take days to find it.''

Mr. Brady shined his light around the roof of the cave. ''Rick, you said some bats flew around you by the waterfall. They probably came from here. They probably go outside through the waterfall shaft.''

Rick looked up at the bats, too. ''You're right,'' he said. ''If we could see where the bats come out, we could go in there. But bats don't go out until night.''

''They flew around when I was shouting for you,'' Janet said. ''That's probably what made them fly in where you were. Maybe if I screamed some more they would fly out. The two of you could go outside. You could see where they come from.''

''Good thinking, Janet,'' Rick said. ''But maybe I should stay down here and shout. It's pretty scary here alone.''

''I know,'' Janet said. ''But I think I can handle it. You and Mr. Brady know more about the cave. You would know where to watch for the bats.''

Rick took her hand. ''You're really something, Janet. OK, give us time to get outside.

Then start screaming.'' He turned to Mr. Brady. ''Let's go.''

They started into the tunnel that led outside. Mr. Brady stopped to ask, ''You sure you're all right, Sis?''

Janet wanted to run after them. But she waved her light and said, ''I'm sure.''

''We'll leave Rick's rope,'' Mr. Brady said. ''Then you can find your way out if you need to.''

He turned back to the tunnel. He and Rick were soon out of sight.

Janet kept her light on. But she didn't look up at the bats. She looked at the tunnel instead. She could go out there soon. "Soon," she said aloud. Her voice sounded hollow in the cave.

She waited until she thought Rick and Mr. Brady were outside. Then she started to scream. It made her feel better to scream.

The noise woke the bats. They flew around the cave. Their strange noises were as loud as her screaming. They were all around Janet. She closed her eyes. That way she couldn't see them.

It seemed like a hundred years before Rick came back.

"It worked, Janet," he said. "A big cloud of bats came out of a hidden opening. We never would have found it without you and the bats."

"Do you think it will lead to the crawl?" Janet asked.

"We'll find out," Rick said.

"Let's get out of here," Janet said. "I hope I never have to look at another bat."

Rick picked up his rope as they went out. When they were outside, he untied it from the little tree.

Janet wasn't surprised to see it was still raining. When they got to where Mr. Brady waited, she saw that he was wet. He had put the package of blankets on a ledge to keep dry.

"I'm ready to go down and see what I can find," Mr. Brady said. He tied his rope around himself. "Let me take your rope, too, Rick. If I find your friends, I'll need one for them to come up on."

Rick looked at him. "Do you think it might be better if I went down? We need someone up here who can pull everyone up. I'm not sure I can do it."

Mr. Brady thought about it. "I guess you're right, Son. I'll stay up here and pull you back." He took off the rope.

Janet watched. Mr. Brady tied both ropes around Rick. He put the rope down around his legs. Then up over his shoulders. It was like a harness. He tied the shovel on Rick's back.

"Keep both ropes on you until you find one of the boys," he said. "Then take one off and put it on him. Yank the rope hard when you want me to pull."

"Right," Rick said. "I'm ready to go now."

Rick pushed through the opening. Mr. Brady wrapped the ropes around a nearby tree. Janet took hold of the ropes behind him. They let them out, inch by inch. Rick went down a long way.

Then they felt a hard yank on the ropes.

"Do you think he has found somebody already?" Janet asked.

Mr. Brady started pulling. "I don't know," he said.

Janet helped him pull. Pretty soon Rick was back outside with them.

"I think I found the crawl," he said. "But the opening is too narrow. I can't get through."

"Did you try to make it bigger with the shovel?" Mr. Brady asked.

"Yes," Rick said. "I can't dig from the outside. There is a little ledge to stand on there. But when I started digging I fell off."

"Then what are we going to do?" Janet asked.

"We'll have to take the time to go get someone smaller. He can get inside and find the guys. Then they can all make the opening bigger from the inside. Then Charlie and Steve can get out."

"But won't it take a long time to get someone?" Janet asked.

"Yes," Mr. Brady said. "So we better go right now."

Janet took a deep breath. "No," she said. "I'll go down there."

Rick and Mr. Brady looked at her. "You can't do that, Janet," Rick said.

Janet put her chin up. "Why not?" she asked. "You did it."

"You just can't, that's all," Rick said.

"Do you think I'm small enough to get through?" Janet asked.

"You could get through the opening all right," Rick said. "But you have to go down next to the waterfall. It's wet and slippery and scary."

"Rick," Janet said. "My brother is somewhere down there. And Charlie is in that crawl. If we don't find them soon, they may die. Isn't that right?"

Rick didn't look at her. But he said "Yes."

"Then I'm going down," she said.

Rick looked at Mr. Brady. "What do you say? Can we let her go?"

Mr. Brady didn't look happy about it. But he said, "I guess she is the only one of us who can get through into the crawl."

Janet tried not to think. Rick and Mr. Brady tied the ropes around her. They tied the little shovel on her back. Then she took her light. She went through the opening to the shaft.

"I'll see you soon," she said.

She started down into the deep, dark hole.

CHAPTER **8**

DOWN THE ICY WATERFALL

It was easy going at first. The shaft didn't slant down too much. Janet shined her light ahead. She stepped carefully over the rocks. She moved forward.

Suddenly the shaft went almost straight down. She had to hang onto the rope. Then she had to go down backward. That was scary. But she could feel Rick and Mr. Brady on the other end of the rope. They gave it out to her a little at a time.

Janet could hear the waterfall. She could feel how cold it was. But she couldn't see it.

Suddenly she was right above it. The water came out of a small tunnel just below her. It splashed out from the edge. Then it fell into the darkness. Icy cold drops of water splashed her.

She had to go down right next to the

waterfall. She had to be very careful not to slip into it.

She didn't let herself think about it. She just kept going down.

Rocks rolled from under her feet as she went. They dropped to the bottom of the waterfall. She wondered how far down they fell. The ropes kept her from falling, too. But what if they should break? What if Rick and Mr. Brady let go?

Janet laughed at herself. Rick and Mr. Brady wouldn't let go. That was one thing she didn't have to worry about. But there were things she did worry about. Like what she might find in the crawl. What would she do if something awful had happened to Charlie? And what if Steve were not there?

Janet remembered what Mr. Brady had said. "Don't think up bad things before they happen."

She shined her flashlight down into the darkness. There was the narrow ledge Rick had found. And there was the opening to the crawl.

Soon she was standing on the ledge. She looked at the opening. She wondered if it were big enough. Could she get through?

She took the shovel from her back. She pushed it ahead of her into the hole. Then she got down on her hands and knees. She pushed herself through. She could just make it.

Her light showed her that she was in a small cave. The icy waterfall nearby made it very cold in there.

She shined her light around. She saw that two tunnels came into the cave. One was very small. The other was larger. She could walk into it if she bent over.

Charlie had said the crawl was bigger after he passed the rock. Janet went into the bigger tunnel.

"Steve!" she shouted. "Charlie!"

She heard a weak sound. She couldn't hear any words, but it seemed like a voice.

She went back and got the shovel. Then she went farther into the tunnel. The ropes moved along behind her.

Janet stopped and shouted again. This time she knew it was a voice that answered. It wasn't too far away. She went faster.

"Get me out of here," she heard a weak voice say.

It didn't take Janet long to get to him. It was Charlie. He was partly buried in dirt.

"Get me out of here," he said again.

"I'll dig you out, Charlie," Janet said. "I have a shovel."

She got up close to him. There wasn't too much room to move. She set her light on a rock and began digging.

More dirt fell down as fast as she dug.

"Get me out of here," Charlie cried. "The roof fell on me. I couldn't get out. It was so dark. And cold."

"Take it easy, Charlie," Janet said. "I'll have you out in a few minutes."

She decided she would have to dig just around his body. She didn't want to cause another cave-in. It might bury them both.

Carefully she dug around him.

Charlie kept talking. "I yelled. No one answered. I didn't think anyone was ever going to come."

"Charlie," Janet said, "listen to me. The dirt keeps falling down. I'm going to push back as much as I can. Then I want you to try to pull yourself out."

"I can't get out," Charlie cried.

Janet pushed at the dirt around his legs. "Yes, you can, Charlie. Just try. Now!"

Charlie tried to pull himself forward. Then

he was out. He started crawling off into the darkness.

"Wait for me," Janet said. She picked up the light and followed Charlie. Just then another big piece of the roof fell in behind them.

They kept going until they were in the small cave that led to the waterfall.

"How do we get out of here?" Charlie sounded scared.

Janet took hold of his arm. "I'll show you soon. But first we have to see if Steve is anywhere near here."

"He isn't here," Charlie said. "Let's go." He saw the small opening Janet had come through. He tried to go over to it.

Janet held onto his arm. "Charlie, don't! You'll fall into a hole if you go out there. You have to tie the rope around you. And we have to make the opening bigger."

Charlie was almost crying. "Janet, we are trapped in here! We can't get out!"

It was just as Rick had said. Charlie was very cold and he wasn't thinking clearly.

"It's OK," Janet told him. "I'll show you how to get out. But first tell me about the gum wrapper you found."

"The gum wrapper?" Charlie asked. Then he seemed to remember. He reached into his pocket. "You mean this gum wrapper?"

He held it out to the light. It was from a stick of spearmint gum. Anyone could have dropped it.

But it was new. And spearmint gum was Steve's favorite.

"He's been here," Janet said. "I know he has."

Charlie looked around. "He's not here now. Let's go."

Janet pointed her light at the narrow little tunnel. "I haven't been in there yet. I think we should check it."

She went over to the small, dark hole. She put down her shovel. She lay down flat. "I'll have to slide in," she said.

"Don't stay very long," Charlie said. "I can't handle it without a light right now."

"I won't be long," Janet said.

She pushed the light ahead of her into the tunnel. "Steve!" she called.

The walls of the tunnel were tight around her. It was scary. She was just about to go back out. Then she saw the boots. She couldn't see much. But she knew they were Steve's boots.

"Steve!" she called. "Are you all right?"

Steve didn't answer.

She moved close to the boots. She took hold of one and shook it.

"Steve," she said. "Talk to me. Are you okay?"

Steve didn't move. He didn't say anything. He was caught in the small space. And he lay still. As if he were dead.

CHAPTER 9

IN DARKNESS AGAIN

Janet set down her light. She took hold of Steve's boots. She tried to pull. But she couldn't pull and move backward in the little tunnel at the same time.

She was afraid. She couldn't get Steve out. Maybe she was trapped in there, too. She began to scream. She tried to move backward. She *was* stuck!

"Charlie!" she screamed.

But Charlie wasn't thinking too well. He wouldn't be much help.

"Stay cool now, Janet," she told herself. "You have to think."

She lay still. She thought about what she had to do. Then slowly she backed out of the little tunnel.

Charlie was waiting for her. "Steve wasn't there, was he? Now we can go." He started toward the opening where they could get out.

Janet stopped him. "Wait! Steve *is* in there. I have to go back in. I'll tie a rope onto him. Then we'll pull him out."

Charlie looked scared. "Why can't he get out by himself?"

"I don't know," Janet said. "There is something wrong with him."

She untied one of the ropes from herself. Then she went back into the crawl. She pulled the rope with her. She tied it around Steve's feet. Then she backed out again.

"Now we'll take hold of the rope and pull," she told Charlie.

They both pulled on the rope. Nothing happened. Steve was caught.

"Take it easy for a minute," Janet told Charlie. "Then we'll try again."

This time Steve began to slide out. "Take it slow," Janet said. "There are rocks on the floor. We don't want to hurt him."

Carefully they pulled Steve out. As soon as he was in the cave, Janet turned him over. There was blood on his face. His eyes were closed.

Janet shook his shoulders. "Steve," she said. "Are you all right?"

Steve didn't move. He didn't say anything.

"Is he dead?" Charlie whispered.

Janet put her ear on Steve's chest. She could hear his heart beating.

"I think he just got so cold he passed out," Janet said. "He isn't wet. But we have to warm him up." She pulled Steve's boots off. "Charlie, you rub his feet. I'll rub his face and hands and arms."

They both rubbed Steve. But he still didn't move.

"We have to do more than this," Janet said. She untied the second rope from her body. She wrapped her raincoat around Steve.

"Charlie," she said, "you take the shovel. Go make that opening bigger. Then we'll have Rick and Mr. Brady pull you up out of here. You can tell Rick to bring the blankets down here. They will help Steve warm up."

Before Charlie started to dig, Janet untied the rope from Steve's boots. She tied it around Charlie like a harness. While Charlie dug, Janet kept rubbing Steve.

The opening was finally big enough. Janet told Charlie to give the rope two hard yanks. "That will tell Rick and Mr. Brady to start pulling," she said.

"I have to have a light," Charlie said. "I can't go up without a light."

"Here, take mine," Janet said. "I won't need it."

Charlie took the light. He disappeared out of the opening. Janet was in the dark again. But she didn't need light to rub Steve.

"It won't be long now, Steve," she told him. "Just hang on a little longer."

Steve didn't move.

A long time went by. Then Janet heard Rick outside the opening. "I'm coming, Janet," he said. "Are you all right?"

"Yes," Janet called. "But I'm not sure about Steve."

"I brought the blankets," Rick said. He pushed them into the cave. Then he came in with two lights. He untied the blankets. He wrapped them around Steve. Then he felt Steve's neck.

"His pulse seems pretty strong," he said.

They sat there beside Steve. Finally he began to wake up. He opened his eyes and said, "It's so cold. I couldn't get out."

"It's OK," Rick said. "Janet got you out."

"Janet?" Steve said. "What is Janet doing here?"

Rick smiled. "Saving your life. That's what Janet is doing here."

"Wow," Steve said. "She is some great sister."

Rick looked at Janet. "She is some great girl!" he said.

Janet smiled. Rick's words had made her feel warm and happy.

Soon Steve felt better. Rick and Janet wrapped a rope around him and sent him up.

"It's your turn now, Janet," Rick said. He helped her tie the rope around herself. Before she stepped out on the ledge, he hugged her. "Just for luck," he said.

The trip back up was harder than the one going down. But it wasn't as scary. Janet was glad to get out of the cave. She was surprised to see that the rain had stopped. The sun was beginning to shine.

Mr. Brady had a small fire burning. Steve and Charlie sat next to it. They were trying to get warm. Janet was glad to see they were all right.

Everyone was there now—everyone but Rick.

"How is Rick going to get back up?" Janet asked. "Both the ropes are up here."

"I'm going down after him," Mr. Brady said. "Just as soon as these young men are strong enough to pull us up."

Janet thought about that. Steve and Charlie didn't look too strong right now. Rick might have to stay down there for a while.

But if *she* went back down for him, he would be out very soon.

She didn't want to go back into the cave. Now she knew what it was like. But she also knew that sometimes there are things you have to do. It doesn't matter if you're afraid. You do them anyway.

"I'll take the rope down to Rick," she said. "Then we'll all go to the car. I've got a picnic basket there. I bet it will be the best meal we ever ate."